Rita, Riley,
and
'Rona Anxiety

A Coronavirus Pandemic Novelette

Novella Jean

Rita, Riley, and 'Rona Anxiety

a coronavirus
pandemic novelette
by

Novella Jean

For my mom,
my sister,
and my aunt.

And our many discussions about masks.

Rita

As Rita sipped her second cup of coffee for the morning, she went over her grocery list—not only to make sure she had everything she needed written down but also to make sure it was in the proper order. She had mapped out her route around the store to ensure the quickest trip possible so she would be in and out with the least amount of exposure.

She would have preferred to have her groceries delivered, of course, to eliminate risk altogether, but she had given up on that option about two months into the pandemic. Half the time the items she requested were out of stock and had been replaced with "similar" items for which she had no use:

peppercorn seasoning in place of bell peppers and corn on the cob, canned corn in place of corn tortillas, and one time even a discounted chew toy for dogs that looked like a tangerine in place of the actual tangerines she had requested. And the produce they picked out for her was the worst: neon green bananas, old potatoes that were sprouting, apples with so many bruises she had to throw them out. She had learned the hard way too many times that she just could not trust others to do her shopping. She always ended up with the products stores couldn't move.

She checked the clock—she had this all timed perfectly. The kids had just started their schooling online, thankfully without any technical difficulties, and were situated in the living room; her husband had just signed into work and was sitting at the kitchen table. They would be okay without her for a little over two hours.

She put her coffee down, unfinished, for she had planned that out as well. She knew exactly how much she could drink (and when) so that she would not need to use a public restroom.

She pulled out her phone and checked the map to see how busy the store was. The algorithm showed: *"not busy."* Perfect.

She checked her covid bag to make sure she had everything: disinfecting wipes, aerosol disinfectant spray, tissues, cough drops (she had found that sucking on one with menthol in the middle made it easier to breathe while wearing a mask), an unopened pack of nitrile gloves, hand sanitizing gel in a pump dispenser situated so she could easily slide her hand in the bag and access it but also situated in a way so nothing would press on the pump (but a plastic bag lined the bottom of the bag, just in case, for she had already ruined two other totes with sanitizing gel), a pack of unused disposable surgical masks, and her UV light wand.

Then, she put on her vest with many pockets and placed her items in it for convenience: a small bottle of hand sanitizer in one pocket (in case she got separated from her covid bag), an extra mask in another pocket, her credit card in another pocket, her ID in another pocket, and her phone in another pocket. Over the months of the pandemic, she had developed a system whereby she could access each item in a way that would not contaminate it, but if she did accidentally touch one of them before sanitizing her hands, then that item would not contaminate other items because it was in its own pocket.

She also had a system for when she came home from the store, so she went about the house making sure everything was ready for her return. She checked to make sure her slippers were next to the front door, which she would change into as soon as she returned so that any virus particles on her shoes would not get into the house. She checked the bins by the front door to make sure they were empty and that there were enough disinfecting wipes next to them. After changing into her slippers, she would wipe down her shoes and covid bag with disinfecting wipes and then wipe down each item from the store and place each one into the bins while it was being decontaminated. (The directions for the disinfecting wipes stated to let it sit for ten minutes.) She would then set the timer next to the bins for ten minutes and then wipe it down with disinfectant as well.

While the items were in the bins, she would carefully go down to the basement—this was the trickiest part of the ordeal because she had to make sure her clothes did not touch anything on the way down—and remove her clothes and put them in the washing machine.

Then, she would put on her clean robe that was on the hook next to the dryer and go upstairs to quickly shower, making sure to take her robe off in a way such that the inside, which had touched her and therefore might be contaminated, would be rolled up so that when she exited the shower she would not touch the potentially contaminated inside part.

After showering, she would put on a new robe, take the potentially contaminated robe down to the basement and place it with all her other potentially contaminated clothes in the washing machine, add soap, and wash them immediately.

Then, she would go back to the front door and wipe down all the items in the bins with a paper towel soaked with water, dry each item, and put them away. She had perfected this routine so that when she went back to the front door it was almost always exactly when the timer would go off. After putting everything away, she would then go back upstairs and get dressed.

After checking to make sure everything was in place for her return, she used the restroom, checked with her kids and husband to make sure they would still be okay in her absence, and then pulled out her masks to choose one to wear. There was the one that showed a caricature of President Trump that said, "Let's get out of this circus. Vote out the clown." There was the navy blue one with the message, written in big, bold, white letters, "I'M WEARING THIS MASK FOR YOU. YOU'RE WELCOME." But in the end, she chose the black one that said "mask it or casket" in a cute font displayed within a cartoon coffin.

Truthfully, the cloth masks really only served the purpose of covering up or distracting people from seeing the N95 mask that she wore underneath, for which she had many times been shamed and glared at for not saving for medical workers working on the front lines.

After securing her two masks over her chin, mouth, and nose, she sprayed her glasses with anti-fog spray and put them on.

Finally, just before exiting, she pulled a new plastic face shield out of its plastic wrap and adjusted the elastic band over the top of her head.

Rita looked out the window to see if the sidewalk was busy. The coast was clear.

She pulled out her phone to request a ride on her rideshare app.

Prior to the request, she had to agree to the new terms:

(1) All windows will be rolled down if possible;

(2) All drivers and passengers must wear a mask;

(3) No more than two passengers per rideshare request;

(4) If there is only one passenger, then the passenger must sit in the back seat on the passenger side farthest away from the driver;

(5) Passengers must maintain as much distance as possible and not lean forward to talk with the driver.

She accepted the terms, requested a ride, and went outside to wait on the stoop of her brownstone.

Riley

It was a miracle. All three children had logged on, signed in, checked in, and were "attending" their online classes, without a single hitch.

Just as Riley was marveling at the sight of her kids at the kitchen table, her husband walked in and said, "My meeting's over, so make all the noise you want."

"When's your next meeting?" Riley asked.

"Not for a couple of hours," he said, pouring himself another cup of coffee.

Riley said, "Hold that thought," and checked her work laptop. There was nothing for which she was currently needed, and she would not be needed at her computer for at least a few more hours.

The stars had aligned. The timing was perfect.

Looking at her family, she declared, "I'm going to the store."

To her kids, she said, "Pay attention to your teachers, and leave each other alone."

To her husband, she said, "Text me anything you can think of that you need."

She ran upstairs and quickly combed her hair, lightly styled it, and threw on a bit of makeup to look halfway decent. She changed out of her yoga pants and t-shirt, wiggled into a pair of stretchy jeans—this pandemic had not been kind to her thighs, but she refused to buy new clothes so she would be motivated to lose the "quarantine fifteen" when all this was over—and threw on a blouse. Running back downstairs, she slipped on her shoes and fished through her purse to make sure she had the wadded-up disposable surgical mask she had been wearing throughout this pandemic. She stuffed it into her pocket, just in case someone made her wear it. Most people didn't have the balls to confront her; she assumed that was because they assumed she had a legitimate medical excuse for not wearing it. She could deal with the bajillion glares she had received over the months, but every now and then there was that one jackass who threatened to throw her out of a store if she didn't mask up.

She grabbed her purse, a jacket, and a handful of reusable bags. She yelled "Love you!" to her family as she opened the front door and requested a ride on her rideshare app as she descended the stairs to the sidewalk.

There were some kind of updated terms she had to agree with, so she clicked "Agree" to get them off the screen so she could request a ride. She looked up to see someone in a coat, scarf, and hat, glaring at her with wide eyes above their mask as they walked out into the street to avoid being near her.

Waiting at the foot of the stairs of her brownstone, she crossed her arms and hugged herself. It was freezing. But between the car and the store, she didn't plan on being outside for long.

Rita

When her ride stopped on the street in front of her, Rita hesitated before getting in.

The driver rolled down the window and asked through a mask, "Are you Rita?"

"Yes, but aren't the windows supposed to be down?"

The driver lowered the windows, and Rita pulled her ginormous covid bag down from her shoulder as she approached the back door on the passenger side. After opening the door, she slid her hand into her covid bag, got a pump of sanitizing gel, and rubbed it onto her hands. Then, she used her UV light wand to decontaminate the area before she got in.

The driver glanced back at her and then did a double take.

"Ma'am, could you put that away, please?" he asked.

"This will only take a minute," Rita responded.

"That thing is a cancer stick. You know that's UV light, right? The reason we wear sunscreen and why tanning bed manufacturers went out of business?"

"It's barely any exposure. It's not going to give you cancer."

"Maybe not cancer, but people have already reported permanent eye damage. You can't just shine UV light around. It's dangerous. Now, please, turn it off or kindly step away from my car."

Taken aback, Rita turned off the wand but did not immediately get in the car. She put the wand back into her bag and reached for the disinfectant spray, just as the car behind them started honking.

"Ma'am, please just get in," her driver said. As she sat down, he pointed at the hand sanitizer he had affixed to the center console in the back seat. "You're welcome to use as much of that as you feel is necessary."

"Oh, I have my own," Rita said, sliding her hand into her covid bag and pumping some sanitizing gel into her palm. She rubbed it onto her hands before putting on her seatbelt, after which she slid her hand into her bag and applied another pump of sanitizing gel.

As he released his foot from the brake and began to drive, her driver said, "I only have the windows up between rides to keep the heat in."

Rita put her head out the window. With the heat on, moist particles in the air carrying the virus would be trapped inside the confined space and might penetrate her masks.

She rubbed hand sanitizer from her covid bag onto her hands before tightening the elastic band of her face shield to prevent it from flying off in the wind.

Once they were on a road with fewer traffic lights, the driver started rolling up the other three windows.

"Hey!" Rita shouted.

"I'm not rolling them up all the way," her driver clarified.

"*All* the windows are supposed to be rolled down *all the way*," said Rita.

"Ma'am, it's forty degrees outside," her driver pleaded.

"Then you should be wearing a coat, gloves, scarf, and a hat," Rita argued.

"Look, ma'am, I drive all day, and it's just too cold to keep the windows down all the way. Having them a quarter of the way down provides plenty of airflow."

"It does not," Rita said.

"It's not *that* big of a deal, anyway," her driver argued. "Don't you realize that? I mean, in the last nine months, less than five percent of the population has even contracted the disease, and less than two percent of those people have died from it. Overall, your risk of death really isn't that high compared to a lot of other viruses. Remember SARS? And MERS? MERS had, like, a thirty percent death rate."

"Those weren't nearly as contagious as SARS-CoV-2 is," Rita informed him. "And anyway, percentage of deaths isn't the problem. The problem is how many people are hospitalized."

"Yeah," her driver said, "but only a small percent of the population has been hospitalized, so even your risk of ending up in the ICU is really low."

"That's not the point." Rita was ready for this. "It's not for your own protection that you wear a mask, or stay six feet away from people, or avoid going out and gathering in large groups. You do it for others, for the—"

"Yeah, for the vulnerable populations, the elderly and immunocompromised," her driver cut in.

"Well, yes, for them, too," Rita continued, "but I was talking about people who might need to go to the hospital for other reasons. What if your father has a heart attack or your mother falls and breaks her leg or your kid gets appendicitis? Then, you take them to the ER, but the hospital has to turn them away because they don't have enough room or staff due to all the COVID patients they have to care for."

At this point, her driver rolled all the windows all the way down, not to decrease risk of exposure because her argument made sense, but to further drown out the noise of her already muffled preaching.

"Think about all the people," Rita continued, "not just your family, who could be in that situation. And you—you drive for a living. Your risk of getting in a car accident is much higher than the average citizen simply because you're on the road so much longer, but if the hospitals are full of COVID patients, then they might have to turn you away if you get injured in an accident."

"I guess you're right," her driver said in a way that signaled the end of the conversation and that it was time to move on to a new topic.

But Rita continued. "And it's not just for the patients but for all the people who work in medical facilities, too. We need all of the people who work at hospitals, and we need them to be healthy, alert, and able to do their jobs. But those poor people have been totally taken for granted and taken advantage of by our society. They've pulled endless all-nighters, worked shifts on end—all while wearing extra PPE that they don't normally wear, like masks, gloves, face shields, and gowns. People complain about wearing a mask, but some medical workers have shown scars on their faces from mask chafing. Not to mention all the deaths they've seen."

"It's their job," her driver mumbled, not loud enough for Rita to hear. He was beginning to regret his own choice of profession.

"And they're positively overwhelmed," Rita continued. "We'll be lucky if we have any medical professionals at all once this is over. They're all so burnt out that they're going to quit. And then we'll have a new crisis on our hands. Hospitals are already reporting that some are quitting. We as a society are truly treating these people horribly. They should be getting honors and medals for their work. They're saving us and keeping this pandemic from being so much worse than it is. It's because of them that you get to say 'it's not so bad,' so it's because of them that you should do your part to make sure it stays 'not so bad.' And just to be a decent human being so they're not so overwhelmed."

Rita leaned her head out the window and took a deep breath, having been careful not to breathe too much when she had been facing the interior of the car while talking.

She pulled her head back in and said, "So, you see, the point is to decrease the spread, not just so you yourself don't get it or even for the people around you, but for everybody."

"Yeah, I agree with you, ma'am, but sometimes don't you think people are blowing it just a little bit out of proportion? I mean, like I said, it's not *that bad* of a virus compared to the others."

Rita couldn't believe it. It was like he hadn't heard a word she'd said!

"Again," she reiterated, "it's not about you risking your own health. It's about being considerate of others."

"But I have to consider myself, too, right?" he said. "It's not healthy to breathe in all those microplastics in masks."

"Surgeons wear masks for hours at a time, several days a week, for years, and they have never reported any issues," Rita argued.

Pointing at his own cloth mask, her driver asked, "Well, what about all the lint I'm breathing into my lungs?"

"You sleep on a cloth pillowcase, don't you?" Rita asked, resisting the urge to inform him of all she knew about how cloth masks were not nearly as effective as surgical masks.

"My pillow doesn't cover my face," her driver said.

"But your mouth is right next to it, wide open, breathing it in for eight hours every night for your whole life. If you can do that, you can wear a mask for a little while. And if you can't, they make hypoallergenic masks."

"Well, you have an answer for everything, don't you," her driver said with sarcasm.

Rita couldn't believe this guy! "Well, yes I do, in fact," she said, "because there's no excuse not to follow the rules to make sure we're all safe."

"From what?" he asked. "It's not that big of a risk."

Rita's jaw would have dropped, had it not been so tightly bound by her masks. She leaned forward and said with emphasis, *"The hospitals are becoming overcrowded."*

"Excuse me, ma'am, you're not supposed to lean forward," he said.

"I'm sorry," Rita quickly said, embarrassed and shaken that she had failed to see her own oversight and lax behavior. She immediately sat back and put her face in the open window.

Then, she continued, saying, "Not to mention—"

"We're here," her driver said, interrupting her as he pulled up to the designated rideshare drop-off location at the curb.

Before getting out, Rita finished, saying, "We just don't know how someone will be affected, if they will die or be asymptomatic or something in between. So it's best to just do everything you can to decrease the spread so more lives aren't needlessly lost to this. We all have to do our part."

"Okay," her driver said.

When Rita said, "Have a good day," as she exited the car, the driver ignored her and drove off as soon as her door was shut.

Riley

A sign taped to the back of the headrest of the front passenger seat read, "PLEASE DO NOT SPRAY DISINFECTANT IN MY CAR."

Upon seeing the sign as she got in, Riley joked, "I bet you get all sorts of crazies—"

"Ma'am," her driver interrupted, "do you have a mask?"

"Oh—yes," Riley said, but she did not put it on.

"It's company policy," her driver said. "You and I both have to wear one."

"What, are they spying on you through the camera in your phone now? I know they track the GPS signal to make sure you're doing the routes correctly."

"No, but we are in the midst of a pandemic."

"Well, I know that," Riley said, "but—"

"Ma'am, please, if you don't wear a mask, I'm going to have to cancel the ride."

"Fine," Riley said, pulling the mask out of her pocket.

Once her mask was on and her seatbelt was fastened, her driver released his foot from the brake and started driving to the store.

Before they reached the end of the block, Riley started rolling her window up and asked, "Can you close the windows? It's freezing in here."

"Ma'am, it's company policy that I have to keep all the windows down."

It was then that Riley noticed how many layers he was wearing: a hat, scarf, coat, gloves, and even a blanket over his lap.

"Well, can I use your blanket, then?"

"No," he said. "That would not be a good idea."

"Then you should have a spare one back here for your customers."

"That would not be a good idea, either," he said again.

"Why not?"

"Because we're in the middle of a pandemic. We can't share things like blankets that could spread the virus."

"Well, we're sharing this car," Riley argued.

With an annoyed sigh, her driver said, "That's why we have to keep all the windows down and wear masks and not do dumb things like share blankets or other objects. I used to have phone chargers and candy in the back seat, but I had to remove all that so there would be less risk of exposure."

As he said it, he started rolling Riley's window back down.

"Hey!" Riley exclaimed, pressing the button to roll the window back up.

"Ma'am, you have to keep the window down," he said. "It's for your own protection."

For nearly a minute the struggle went on, with the window moving up and down.

"Ma'am, please, you are going to break it."

Riley looked at him and said, "Then stop lowering my window and let me just keep it up. I'm freezing back here."

While she was talking, Riley had stopped pressing the button. Her driver lowered the window all the way and activated the window lock.

"Are you kidding me?" she exclaimed as she tried to raise the window again.

"Ma'am, it's company policy. If you really feel that strongly about it, I can drop you off here and cancel the ride."

Riley huffed as she sat back in her seat and crossed her arms, hugging herself to stay warm.

"Really," her driver said, "it's not that much they're asking of us. We're a bunch of sissies if we can't handle wearing a mask when we go out. It's not like we're trapped in our homes. If Anne Frank could spend two years in an attic, we can limit our outings and wear a mask when we do go out. We have online shopping and things delivered directly to us, streaming services with endless hours of entertainment. And we can actually go out. Anne Frank couldn't."

"Yeah, because she had Nazis patrolling the streets telling everyone what to do," Riley argued. "We can go out now, but if this continues, we'll be stuck in our attics, too. Is that how you want to live?"

"Wow," her driver said, "that's not even close to the reason why she was hiding."

"It's not far off from how we are now," Riley said.

"Are you kidding?" he asked. "It's way far off."

"Think about it," Riley said. "At first, they said a month. That was eight months ago. How long is this going to go on? And now they say wear a mask, but what next? And some places have a curfew, like the virus is a vampire and only comes out at night. They're treating us like we're children who can't take care of ourselves. You say we can go out now, but if we continue to let them put these restrictions on us, it's only a matter of time before they will be literally locking people up in their homes. And people look at us like we're crazy for saying it's a dictatorship, but open your eyes. How do you not see what our country is becoming? Executive orders used to be a rare last resort, but over the last three presidencies, presidents have been signing more and more executive orders, just because they don't get their way with Congress. And now the current president is allowing governors to arrest citizens for having people over in their own homes! When will people see what's happening to the republic and our freedom? Why don't people see where this is going, that if we allow this to happen and if we get used to this happening, then they'll just keep tightening the reins until we live in a regressed world of kingship and feudalism? That's where this is going. They want us to be mindless automatons that just do whatever they say."

Her driver was about to say something, but Riley continued before he could interject. "And did you hear Biden in that one debate? He said, '*I am the democratic party,*' like a dictator. Don't get me wrong, I voted for him, but apparently acting like a dictator has become so normal to us that we had to choose between two for our next four years. We'll have to watch him like a hawk."

Just as she was finishing up her rant, the car slowed to a crawl and then stopped, stuck in traffic. Another car also stopped in the lane next to her. Being another rideshare, all the windows were down, and two passengers were in the back seat.

Riley pointed at the car and said, "See, since my window is down, I'm now less than six feet away from this person, and I'm completely exposed and unable to prevent myself from breathing the same air as they are because you won't let me roll my window up to protect myself."

"I thought breathing the same air didn't bother you," he said.

"It doesn't, but if you truly believed what you said about having my window rolled down for my own protection, then you would want my window rolled up in this case for my protection right now."

The passenger in the other car, being so close, had heard Riley and said, "It's only for a minute or so. And with all this wind between our two cars, you're much safer keeping the window open than keeping it closed."

"Well, I know it's not that big of a deal," Riley said to the passenger in the other car. "It's this lunatic driving me that cares so much and feels so strongly about the windows."

"That's really nice of him to be so considerate of your safety," the passenger in the other car said.

Riley's jaw dropped, causing her mask to slip down below her nose. But before Riley could argue, traffic had moved, and the other car sped off.

"Ma'am," her driver said, "can you please raise your mask above your nose?"

Riley glared at him when she met his eyes in the rearview mirror.

In an exaggerated gesture, she adjusted her mask. Then, she said, "It doesn't matter, anyway. I'm not infected. I got tested for Thanksgiving, and I was negative, and I feel the exact same now as I did then."

"That doesn't mean anything," her driver said.

"Excuse me," Riley responded, utterly offended, "I've had this body for nearly forty years. I think I would know if I got sick. No government official out there is going to tell me that they know my body better than I do."

"Wow, you are really ignorant."

"*Excuse me*?" Riley said, leaning forward.

"Ma'am, please sit back," her driver said. "It's company policy." After Riley leaned back, he continued, "Do you know what asymptomatic means? It means you have *no* symptoms. You're right that you might know when you're sick, but you can't know if you have a virus if it doesn't cause symptoms. That's the whole point of everyone having to wear a mask, because you don't always know if you've got it and you might give it to someone else who does get sick from it, even if you don't."

"Well, it hardly matters anymore, with the vaccine here."

"It's not here, yet."

"It's already being distributed," Riley informed him.

"It will take months to make enough for everybody, and anyway most people say they aren't even going to get it, so that's a waste. What's going to happen is all these idiots aren't going to get the vaccine, the virus will mutate again, making the vaccine useless, and then we'll be in the midst of a worse pandemic. This is far from over."

"Well, I'm getting the vaccine, that's for sure," Riley declared.

"You will?" her driver asked, looking at her in the rearview mirror with disbelief. He was under the impression that anti-maskers were also anti-vaxxers.

"Of course!" Riley exclaimed. "What made you think I wouldn't?"

"Because you talk like a crazy conspiracy nut," he said.

"*What did you just call me*?" Riley asked. Boy, was she ready to give him a piece of her mind. "Listen, you—"

"We're here," he said, pulling up to the curb.

Once they reached the designated rideshare drop-off location, Riley didn't even wait for the car to come to a complete stop before she unbuckled her seatbelt and started opening the door.

As she exited the vehicle, Riley heard the driver say, "Wear a mask, wash your hands often, and keep your distance," before speeding off.

Rita

Rita slammed the car door shut—her rating be damned. She knew he would give her a one-star review as a passenger, but she didn't care. She would call the company as soon as she got home to tell them what an unsafe driver he was. The nerve of that guy! Like she didn't know anything about the coronavirus or this pandemic. As if he knew *so much more* than she did.

She huffed and slid her hand into her covid bag and pumped some hand sanitizer into her palm without thinking about it. She furiously rubbed the sanitizing gel all over her hands and wrists.

As she approached the shopping carts, Rita pulled out a disinfecting wipe.

"Ma'am, we have wipes over here you can use," an employee by the door offered as she motioned to the provided wipes next to the carts.

"Thank you, but that's okay," Rita replied. Holding the disinfecting wipe, she used it as a shield between her hand and the cart handle as she pulled out a shopping cart. Then, with her other hand, she reached into her covid bag and pulled out her aerosol can of disinfectant spray.

"Oh, ma'am," the store employee said, "those carts have already been sanitized."

"That's all right," Rita said. "I just like to be extra cautious."

"Okay," the employee said, "but, seriously, that's overkill because we've already cleaned them."

Ignoring the employee, Rita sprayed the entire cart down and then went over it with the disinfecting wipe.

As a man grabbed a cart nearby, he joked, "They should hire you to clean these."

Then, he walked right by her—coming within two feet—to go into the store.

"Excuse me!" Rita exclaimed as she leaped away from him.

He continued walking without acknowledging her any further.

Rita looked back at the employee who was still standing by the door and said, "Some people are so rude."

She took her cart and went into the store, careful to keep a six-foot radius around the employee.

She reached into the vest pocket that contained her list and pulled it out. She made her way through the aisles, dodging other people to maintain a six-foot distance.

When she turned down one aisle, there were three people close to her end. An arrow on the floor indicated the direction to walk, so she waited patiently for the people to continue on before she entered.

But then someone pushed by her, ignoring the six-foot distance rule. Upon seeing them, Rita leaped to the side to get as physically far away from them as she could.

"That was really graceful!" they said. "Are you a ballerina?"

She narrowed her eyes at them, but they just laughed and continued shopping.

She waited a little longer. Who were these people, standing there staring at items? So inconsiderate. Didn't they know about the pandemic? Didn't they know the authorities suggested making a list so there would be a constant flow of people so a distance of six feet could always be maintained?

Finally, the people moved, and she was able to enter the aisle.

Once she got to the end of it, a man turned into the aisle and would have run right into her, had she not been standing behind her cart. She glared at him and pointed at the arrow on the floor to let him know he was going the wrong way.

He just shrugged and continued walking past her.

Rita shook her head and turned to go down the next aisle.

This was why she hated shopping so much during this pandemic. Nobody cared about the rules or suggestions. She felt like she was the only one being considerate of others.

As she shopped, after each time she touched an item, she reached into her covid bag, pumped some hand sanitizer into her palm, and rubbed it on both her hands before resuming her shopping. It was another reason she hated shopping during this pandemic: it was such a hassle.

In the next aisle, a woman pulled her mask down below her chin to answer a phone call. Rita glared at her, and when the woman did not readjust her mask, Rita stood right in front of her—still six feet away, of course—and made her eyes as big and wide as she could make them and stared that woman down.

Finally, the woman glanced at her and threw her hands up. "We still have to live our lives," she said to Rita.

Nevertheless, she pulled her mask up over her nose as she said into the phone, "Nothing, I was talking to someone else. Can you still hear me? Because some bitch just glared at me for pulling my mask down so I could be understood, so now I have to yell, which is probably spreading more COVID particles than when I was talking softly without the mask on."

"You don't spread COVID particles," Rita corrected her. "You spread SARS-CoV-2 particles.

COVID's the disease you contract from SARS-CoV-2."

In response, the woman tilted her head from side to side as she gave Rita an exaggerated mock glare before turning around and leaving.

In the next aisle, as Rita was reaching up to get an item off the top shelf, another woman stood on the other side of her cart, almost touching it because she was so close. As Rita put the item in her cart, she purposely nudged it forward, causing it to bump into the woman.

"Excuse me!" the woman exclaimed.

"Well, that wouldn't have happened if you maintained six feet of distance like you're supposed to, would it?" Rita asked her.

"Are you okay?" the woman asked with genuine concern.

"I will be once you're six feet away from me," Rita said.

"Okay, okay," the woman said defensively, taking several steps back. "I'm sorry."

Rita looked down at her list as she continued walking down the aisle. Only two aisles left and then she could leave this hell. She was so sick of how insufferable a simple errand like grocery shopping had become because of all these stupid people.

Just as Rita looked up from her list, another woman pushing a cart turned down the aisle.

"Oops!" she said and started backing away.

"Thank you!" Rita called to her.

"No problem!" the woman replied.

"I think you and I are the only two people left in the world who remember there's still a virus going around," Rita said.

Nodding in agreement, the woman replied, "It seems like everyone else has just decided it's over. But that's not how pandemics work. And I didn't make it this far just to catch it in the end."

"Amen!" said Rita.

Then, standing more than ten feet apart, the two women gave each other an air high five as Rita turned out of the aisle so the other woman could go into it alone.

Finally, Rita had every item on her list and was ready to check out.

However, as she stood in the checkout line, a man started to get in line in front of her.

"Excuse me, sir," she called to him. "I'm in line."

"This line?" he asked, pointing at the one in front of him.

"Yes, this line," Rita said, stretching her hand out in front of her to show how she was in the same path. "We're supposed to maintain a six-foot distance."

"But you prefer a ten-foot distance," he said.

"How tall are you?" Rita asked him.

"How tall am I?"

"Yes, how tall are you?"

"Six-foot-two," he said.

"If you were to lie down on the floor in the space between us, would you fit?" Rita asked.

His eyes narrowed at her, and he said, "All but the top two inches of my head."

As he walked past her to get in line, Rita leaped away and got on the other side of her cart.

"Don't worry," he said, "I'll stay *way back* here." Then, he snorted and shook his head.

"Smartass," Rita mumbled under her breath. She couldn't wait to get out of there.

"Ma'am, you can come forward and start putting your items on the belt," the cashier said to her.

But the customer ahead of her was still at the card machine, which, by Rita's estimate, was only about four feet from where she would be standing if she started unloading her cart.

"That's okay, I'll just wait a minute," Rita said to the cashier.

She heard that man behind her comment, "That's right, we all have all the time in the world to wait on you."

Rita ignored him.

Once Rita was done unloading her groceries onto the belt, she pulled out her aerosol can of disinfectant to clean the card reader.

"Ma'am," the bagger said, "the sign clearly states not to spray the machine."

"But I don't want to touch it after the previous customer," Rita said. "I saw her use it, and it hasn't been disinfected since she touched it."

The bagger said, "There's hand sanitizer right next to it that you can use after you touch it."

Rita glared at him, put her can of disinfectant spray back into her covid bag, pulled out a disinfecting wipe, and brushed it over the buttons of the machine.

The bagger rolled his eyes and shook his head.

Trying to lighten the mood and relieve the tension, the cashier joked, "It's funny how this global pandemic has turned everyone into a germophobe, isn't it?"

"You know the phrase 'global pandemic' is redundant, right?" Rita asked him. "It's like saying PIN number or ATM machine or chai tea or please RSVP. *Pan* means global. A *pan*-demic is a global epidemic."

Blank stare from the cashier.

"Do you want your receipt in the bag?" he asked.

"Of course I do," Rita said. "I don't want to touch it after you've touched it."

"But I touched the bags," the bagger said.

"Just give it to me," Rita said. After she took the receipt from him, she threw it on top of the groceries in one of the bags the bagger had placed in her cart, reached into her covid bag for a pump of hand sanitizer, rubbed the gel all over her hands, and then pushed her cart toward the exit.

Riley

Riley slammed the door shut—her rating be damned. The nerve of that guy telling her how she should live! Like she didn't know anything about the coronavirus or this pandemic. As if he knew *so much more* than she did.

She pulled her mask down and took a few deep breaths of fresh air. As she stood there, other customers going into the store glared at her as they gave her a wide berth when they walked by.

When she was ready, she got a cart, pulled out her phone, and opened the text message from her husband with the list of items he wanted her to get.

She roamed around the store, first getting the non-refrigerated items on his list, then browsing while making meal plans in her mind for the next week and thinking of what ingredients she would need. As she walked, everyone else shuffled away from her to make sure she didn't get too close. See, she didn't have to worry about maintaining physical distance because everyone else did that for her.

When she reached across someone to get an item, she was met with a glare.

When she went down an aisle and then remembered something else, having to move in the wrong direction to go back to the other end, she was met with glares.

Riley imagined this was how citizens in communist Russia felt: told exactly where to stand, which way to walk down the aisle at a grocery store, not allowed to just go where they pleased or make decisions for themselves. And nobody around her seemed to care at all that this was what their world was becoming.

"Ma'am," a woman said to her, "will you please pull your mask up over your nose?"

She had been walking around this whole time with it like this and nobody else had said anything. Riley ignored the woman and continued shopping.

"Ma'am," a man said to her, "you need to keep a distance."

"Oh, come on," Riley said, "get real. There's no way to be distanced in these narrow aisles."

"That's why there are arrows," the man said.

"I don't have time to stand around and wait for people to move," Riley said.

Shaking his head, he gave an irritated grunt as he walked away.

After a bout of several people glaring at her with wide eyes and shuffling around her, she pulled her mask up over her nose. Immediately, her glasses began to fog up. She pulled them out on her nose just a bit.

In the produce section, when she was selecting tomatoes, one guy said, sarcastically, "Touch all of them, why don't you."

Riley replied, "I don't want any with bruises." She picked one up and held it out to him. "See? You want me to just take whatever I touch and end up with crap I have to throw out?"

"We're in a pandemic," he said.

"There's a pandemic?" Riley asked with sarcasm. "I had no idea! Thanks for letting me know."

"Oh, so is that your strategy, then?" he asked, pointing at the tomatoes in front of her. "Touch everything to get the virus everywhere and force us all to get it?"

Riley rolled her eyes and walked away. She would come back when this man was gone. She missed being able to go out and ignore everyone and be equally ignored in return. Now, everyone was painfully aware of everyone else—and not in a good way.

Next to the toilet paper, a sign read, "Please do not hoard items so everyone can have some. We're all in this together!"

Pointing at the sign, Riley snorted and said to a woman standing nearby, "Doesn't feel like we're all in this together, am I right? Feels like *they* are telling *us* how to live our lives." As she spoke, Riley's mask slowly started slipping down and settled just below her nose.

The woman eyed Riley while slowly inching away.

In the next aisle, just as Riley was about to exit, a woman turned into it. Immediately upon seeing Riley, her eyes went wide, her eyebrows shot up, and she backed away.

Like Riley was a mutant. Like there was something wrong with her. Like the world would end if anyone got too close to her.

"I don't bite," Riley joked, but the woman did not respond.

Glares, glares, and more glares—this was how Nazi Germany got started: get the people to police themselves. Next they'd be incentivizing citizens to rat each other out to the secret police.

"Ma'am," a store employee said as he approached her. "We've had some complaints from other customers. I'm going to have to ask you to pull your mask up so it completely covers your nose."

"Complaints from other customers?" Riley asked. "Really, you don't say."

"Ma'am, please," he said, "it's the law. I could lose my job. The store could get fined. If you're not going to follow the rules, I'm going to have to ask you to leave."

"What if I have a medical condition?" Riley asked.

"Then you can take advantage of our curbside pickup service," the employee responded.

"I can't afford to keep a car in this city," Riley said.

"Then, we offer delivery," he responded.

Riley said, "You want me to pay a delivery fee every single time I want to buy something? Times are hard enough as it is, with everyone losing their jobs, and now stores are trying to nickel and dime us out of every last penny we have."

"Either way, ma'am," he said, "I'm going to have to ask you to leave if you don't pull your mask up. It's the law."

"Of course it is," Riley said, pulling her mask up. She had to get groceries, so she had no choice but to comply, but she just couldn't believe what the world was turning into—and that nobody seemed to be bothered by it.

She huffed, sending a wave of breath through the top of her mask, up her face, and fogging up her glasses so completely that she couldn't even see if the employee was still in front of her. She bent her head down and looked over the top of her glasses.

He was gone.

She readjusted her mask so she could breathe again.

Finally, she was done shopping and ready to leave this hell. She got in line to check out.

"Ma'am," the cashier said, "Can you stand back?" He pointed at a sign behind her taped to the floor that read, "Stand here."

"I'm close enough," Riley said.

"Ma'am," the cashier said, "please stand on the designated spot. We're in a pandemic."

"No shit," Riley mumbled under her breath as she took a step backward to stand on the sign. She couldn't wait to get out of there.

As she was checking out, a bagger started putting her groceries in paper bags.

"Oh, I brought my own," Riley told him.

"Ma'am," the cashier said, "we can't allow you to use those in the store. You'll have to bag things yourself outside."

"How am I supposed to carry all these groceries outside when you won't let us take our carts out of the store?" Riley asked.

"You can carry them in these bags and then re-bag them outside," the bagger suggested, continuing to put her groceries in the paper bags and then placing them in her cart.

"So you can get five cents per bag, even though you won't let me use my own?" Riley asked. "Well, that's really convenient. Just like it's convenient for all these companies that make masks that the government forces us to wear."

Blank stare from the cashier.

"Do you want your receipt in the bag?" he asked.

"No, I'll just take it," Riley said, grabbing it from him. Then, she let out an audible exhalation to express her grievance and pushed her cart toward the exit.

The Breaking Point

Standing by her groceries at the designated rideshare pickup location, Rita became aware of someone setting groceries down next to hers and standing less than six feet away.

Riley squatted down and started transferring her groceries from the paper bags the grocery store had forced her to buy to her reusable bags. She pulled her mask down below her chin so she could breathe.

"Excuse me," Rita said to Riley.

Riley looked up at her and said, "Yes?"

Rita said, "You need to put your mask up over your nose and step away. You're too close to me."

"Why don't *you* step away?" Riley asked.

"Because I was here first, and I'm waiting for my ride," Rita said.

"Well, I'm waiting for a ride, too," Riley said, "and since this is where we're supposed to wait, I can't really go anywhere, can I?"

"But you have to step away," Rita said, "and you have to put your mask on."

"We're outside," Riley said.

"That doesn't matter," Rita said, raising her voice.

After Riley finished transferring the groceries, she took the empty paper bags and put them in the recycling bin by the front entrance of the store. When Riley returned to her groceries and pulled out her phone to request a ride, she intentionally stood close to Rita, with her mask still down below her chin.

"I told you to stand over there," Rita told Riley in a loud voice.

A few people around them started to take notice.

"Why don't *you* stand over there?" Riley asked Rita. "I'm not going to move all these bags just because you don't like where I'm standing. If you want more distance between us, then you can move."

Rita took a few steps to be farther from Riley, but there were still people walking around her, getting too close. She looked back at Riley and saw that she still had her mask down below her chin. Rita told her, "You have to put your mask up."

"I can't see with a mask on because my glasses fog up, and we're outside where there's plenty of airflow, so you're plenty protected from me," Riley reasoned.

"These are the rules," Rita said. "For a reason. We're in a pandemic. You're being selfish."

Riley rolled her eyes. "The government is blowing this way out of proportion."

"*Put. Your. Mask. Up,*" Rita said, emphasizing each word.

Riley had had it with this woman. She turned to her and said, "Sorry, I didn't hear you with that restraint you willingly put on your face because you're a scared little lemming that does whatever the government tells you to do."

"*I'm* the one who's afraid?" Rita exclaimed. "You're so scared you believe conspiracy theories just so you can stay in a cozy little world of denial!"

"Conspiracy theories?" Riley laughed. "Please, woman, you don't even know me."

At the start of the commotion, all the people around them started staring. Some pulled out their phones, ready to record, just in case.

"Yes," Rita said, "conspiracy theories that the government is blowing this out of proportion. You said so yourself. You're scared out of your mind, aren't you? That's why you're pretending there's nothing going on and that the pandemic doesn't exist."

Riley stepped closer to Rita and said, "I'm not afraid of anything, especially of getting this stupid virus."

When Riley took another step closer, Rita leaped backward and exclaimed, "Get the hell away from me, you crazy science-denying Karen anti-masker hick!"

As she did so, Rita's arms went flailing upward, knocking off her face shield and revealing a thick indentation across her forehead. The face shield went flying into the air and was carried off in the wind.

Riley yelled back at her, "You fascist Nazis haven't taken over, yet. This is still a free country, and I can stand wherever I please!"

Then, not knowing what came over her, Riley bared her teeth, put her hands up with bent fingers to imitate bear claws, and with a loud growl lunged at Rita.

Rita screamed and in one, quick, involuntary reflex reached into her covid bag, grabbed the aerosol can, and sprayed disinfectant into the air in front of her—which, due to her lunging so close, meant Rita sprayed disinfectant right into Riley's face.

Now everybody had their phones out. They would make a fortune off this video.

Riley screamed and started ferociously swatting the air.

Still armed with her aerosol can, Rita frantically waved it all around her, spraying in every direction, while screaming and leaping away from Riley.

Phones still out, cameras pointed at the scene, the crowd around them backed away—maintaining much more than six feet from the two women so as not to get caught in the crossfire, while also glancing around to make sure they were distanced from each other.

"Stop spraying those toxins!" Riley yelled at her. "You're more dangerous than the virus, you stupid, paranoid bitch!"

Still swatting the air with one hand, Riley reached in front of her with her other hand and ripped off Rita's cloth mask, exposing the N95 mask underneath.

A collective gasp of shock and surprise could be heard from the crowd around them.

"Oh!" Riley exclaimed, looking around at everyone and pointing at Rita. "She called me selfish. Look at her! She's hoarding masks that are supposed to be reserved for medical workers!"

"Give that back!" Rita yelled, reaching for her cloth mask in Riley's hand.

Rita grabbed the mask with one hand and continued wildly spraying disinfectant into the air with her other hand. Riley, still holding onto the mask, bent her other arm ninety degrees at the elbow and waved in a fast windshield-wiper motion in front of her face to protect herself from the disinfectant spray.

The store manager appeared at the door, wide-eyed and unsure of what to do, seeing that this fight was bound to get even more physical. Then, she turned around to the customers who had been ready to exit and told them to go back into the store. Some did as she said, fearful of going outside into the fight. Others stayed at the doorway to watch the show. They put their phones up and started recording. This was the most exciting thing to happen to them since the pandemic began!

The Police Station

Sitting in the back seat of the police car with her hands cuffed behind her, Rita asked, "Can you open this window back here?"

"No," the officer said.

"It's my right to have plentiful airflow. We're in a pandemic," Rita said.

"It's not that big of a deal," the officer said. "Everyone's blowing this way out of proportion. Most people who get it don't even have symptoms."

"That's not the point." Rita was ready for this. "It's not for your own protection that you wear a mask—"

"No, it's not," the officer said, interrupting her. "But the economy is artificially inflated, kids are way behind in school, businesses are failing—all except one, which is thriving. Don't get me wrong, though, I'm glad we already had all that instant online ordering and delivery set up. Can you imagine what this would have looked like if that system hadn't already been in place?—But still, people lost their jobs, domestic violence is up—"

"Well," Rita started.

"Really?" the officer said, interrupting her again. "You want to argue with the cop driving you to a police station while you're trapped in the back seat of her cop car?"

That shut Rita up.

She looked out the window and caught sight of her reflection. There were grainy marks across her forehead where the foam padding of her face shield had been.

"I know what I'm talking about," the officer continued. "Domestic violence is definitely up, and so is child abuse and alcohol and drug abuse. We're going to be paying for these things for *years* to come, just in psychiatric bills alone. And depression is on the rise, not to mention anxiety. They say the vaccine's going to be free for everyone—they should hand out benzos for free until the vaccine is available."

Rita remained silent. Clearly this police officer was an idiot and would not understand what she had to say, anyway.

"And these masks," the officer said, "study after study has shown they don't do that much to protect you from the virus."

The officer continued talking, but Rita couldn't hear her, fuming from thinking about the ignorance of the very people who were supposed to serve and protect the public. All Rita could think about was what she wanted to say, which was that surgeons don't wear masks in the operating room to protect themselves from the patients they're operating on; it's to protect the patients from them. Similarly, *that* was why there was a rule to wear a mask, to protect others, not the wearer. And here was this police officer, in a profession to protect other people, talking about protecting herself instead. How dumb could people be?

*   *   *

Sitting in the back seat of the police car with her hands cuffed behind her, Riley looked out the window and opened her mouth as wide as she could so her mask slipped down below her nose.

"Ma'am, put your mask back up," the officer said from the driver's seat.

"How?" Riley asked. "You handcuffed me."

"You can use your shoulder to push it up, or I can pull over and do it for you," the officer said.

Riley did as she was told, turning her head and brushing her chin down on one shoulder. For once, she was grateful the mask shifted upward and covered the whole lower half of her face. "It's not like a mask does that much, anyway," she said once the mask was back in place.

Well, that was the wrong thing to say.

"It does a lot, actually," the officer said. "Not only to protect other people from a virus you may not know you have but also to show your fellow Americans that you care about them enough to wear a mask. It boosts everyone's morale to know we are a team, working together, and looking out for each other."

"Honestly," the officer continued, clearly exasperated. "I did two tours in Afghanistan. I risked my life, my physical health, and my mental health for my fellow Americans, only to find out that all these Americans I was protecting are willing to risk each other's lives just because they don't want to wear a piece of fabric over their faces. Do you know how much I had to wear on my head and face while I was over there? Not to mention how much all my gear weighed."

"Thank you for your service," Riley said. Then, she added, "I mean that," because she did.

Even so, as the officer continued talking, Riley couldn't hear her because her mind was too occupied thinking about all the things she wanted to say but wouldn't dare say to a veteran, let alone to the officer who was driving her to the police station. She wanted to point out that there were tons of viruses floating around that didn't cause any symptoms and nobody ever wore a mask to protect each other from those. She also wanted to point out that some viruses were even beneficial.

But it was no use. Clearly this police officer was an idiot and would not understand what she had to say, anyway. How dumb could people be?

*   *   *

Having each been lectured at without being allowed to voice their own opinions, it was no surprise that Rita and Riley immediately resumed their argument upon seeing each other in the lobby of the police station.

Quickly, their officers stepped between them.

"Ma'am," Rita's officer said to her, "ma'am, if you don't calm down—"

To Riley, Rita yelled, "You are a danger to society!"

"Ma'am," the officer said to her, "please—"

"You are reckless, rude, and inconsiderate!" Rita continued.

"Ma'am," her officer said.

"You are a bioterrorist!" Rita declared.

"Ma'am, if you don't calm down, I'll have to place you in the drunk tank."

That got Rita's attention.

Now, to the officer, she screamed, "The *drunk* tank!? Do you know what kind of people are in there?"

"Ma'am."

"You can't put me with those people! There's no way to distance in there, and they won't—"

"Ma'am, I'm serious," the officer continued...

Meanwhile, Riley had also been yelling, first at Rita, then to anyone who would listen. "*How am I the only one—*"

"Ma'am," Riley's officer said to her, "please calm down."

"Who sees that we are living in a dictatorship!?"

"Ma'am," her officer said again.

"Even with all the protests this summer," Riley continued.

"Ma'am," her officer pleaded.

"You people are morons. Blind. And completely brainwashed!"

"*Ma'am,*" the officer said, this time in a loud, stern tone...

Then, unable to take it any longer, Rita and Riley both exclaimed, "*STOP MA'AM-ING ME!*"

The entire lobby went quiet.

With heavy exhalation, both Rita and Riley looked around them, as if seeing for the first time just exactly where they were—the spell broken, their respective episodes at a close, reality finally setting in.

When their eyes met, both women looked at each other with stunned expressions.

The two officers looked at each other.

Rita's officer rolled her eyes. "Come on," she said, taking Rita's arm and leading her to the back.

The other officer followed with Riley in tow.

They removed the handcuffs and put them each in a separate holding cell next to each other.

Rita sat on the bench and stared straight ahead of her, still with that same stunned expression on her face. She couldn't believe where she was.

After their officers left, the guard let Riley out and led her to a desk, where she called her husband to let him know what had happened.

Five minutes later, when Riley was done and back in her cell, the guard led Rita to the desk to call her family, too.

As Rita returned, she looked at Riley sitting on the bench in her cell, leaning forward with her elbows on her knees and her chin resting on her clasped hands, just staring at the floor.

By now both women were calm and had returned to their normal selves, feeling equally foolish and ashamed.

After the guard locked the cell door, Rita sat on the bench and leaned her back against the wall with a heavy sigh. "This pandemic is exhausting."

Still staring at the floor with her chin resting on both fists, Riley nodded slowly in agreement.

"I'm just so tired of fighting," Rita said. "I feel like it's just me, up against everything, like nothing is on my side."

"Tell me about it," Riley agreed.

"Like last night, for example," Rita continued, "I spent *two hours* trying to figure out how to upload my kids' homework into this new software program their school just started using and kept getting all these error messages. I finally just called their teachers and asked if I could take pictures with my phone and text them."

"Our school is using this program where they do everything—seriously, *everything*—on these little laptops they gave the kids," Riley said, "and it's just terrible for their eye health. I know because I sit at a computer all day, and I can't imagine what this is doing to them, not to mention all that sitting. You'd think with all these rules that we're a health-conscious society and wouldn't ask our kids to sit so much."

"Especially because obesity is such a big factor with this virus," Rita added.

"I make my kids get up and walk around every twenty minutes," Riley said.

Rita said, "We have a wheel they spin between each class, which is about every forty-five minutes. They put their favorite activities on it, like jumping jacks or cartwheels, and they see how many they can do in a set amount of time. We record it in a notebook, and if they beat their personal best for that activity, they get a prize."

Riley sat up and turned to look at Rita through the bars that separated their cells. "That's a great idea," she said. "I'm going to have to remember that."

Rita shifted on her bench so she faced Riley. "We made the wheel from scratch. It took loads of time, first to list everything they wanted to put on it, then cutting out spokes and putting it together. It took care of at least half a Saturday without having to gear up and venture out."

Riley said, "We've completely run out of things to do at our house. I never dreamed my kids could get sick of watching TV."

Rita laughed out loud. "I know, right?"

"It's not like I want them to be couch potatoes," Riley continued, "but there are a couple of hours here and there when they don't have school but my husband and I have work we have to do, so I let them watch a movie or something. Lately, they don't want to do that, and I feel like I am just running out of options."

"I had to reduce my hours at work to part-time," said Rita. With a sigh, she added, "In theory, we should be able to make it work, timing breaks and everything, but there's just always something that comes up with the kids that has to be fixed or addressed right away. So, I finally told my boss I just couldn't work as many hours."

Riley said, "I was fortunate to be able to shift my hours around so I take a few half-days during the week and make up for the work nights and weekends while my husband takes care of the kids."

"You don't get *any* days off, then?" Rita asked.

"Oh, I've taken some vacation days," Riley replied. "But it's not like I go anywhere or do anything. Seems like a waste."

"It's not," Rita said. "You need time away from work. In fact, a couple nights over the summer, I told my family I was on emergency notice only, went in the bedroom, shut the door, opened a bottle of wine, and just had some time to myself. With how cooped up I had been for months, it was glorious."

"I'll have to give that a try," said Riley.

"I can't recommend it enough," said Rita. "Seriously, I was shocked at how much it actually felt like a real vacation."

Riley pulled the bottom of her mask out away from her chin, careful to keep the rest of the mask covering her mouth and nose. "I just can't breathe with this thing on," she said. "I'm glad most people can, but I don't think they understand that some of us just can't wear masks. And then my glasses fog up, so I can't see anything. I actually started hyperventilating the other day in the middle of a store, and then my glasses were completely opaque. I nearly had a panic attack and just had to rip my mask off right there. And the look this woman gave me—you'd think I had pulled out a gun."

Rita laughed under her breath. Then, she clarified, "I'm not laughing at you. That's horrible that that happened, and I'm sorry masks give you so much trouble. I was just thinking about how many times I've given that look. I know I've given my share of glares."

"Maybe I just got a bad batch of masks or something," Riley said. She *had* been wearing the same one this whole time. She hadn't even tried any others, so maybe there *was* something wrong with this one.

"Oh, there's one brand a friend of mine found that she loves," said Rita. "She had a terrible time finding ones she could breathe in, and she swears by them. I'll text her for the information once we get our phones back and send you the link. And there's an anti-fog spray I use for my glasses. I'll text you the info for that as well."

"Thank you, that would be great," Riley said.

They both sighed and leaned back with their heads against the wall.

"I'm Rita, by the way."

"Riley."

After a few moments of silence, Riley said, "Rita?"

"Yes, Riley?"

"I'm sorry I lunged at you."

Rita turned her head to see Riley through the metal bars between them. She said, "I'm sorry I sprayed you with disinfectant."

Riley snorted. "I deserved it."

Rita started laughing and said, "So did I."

*   *   *

Nearly an hour later, Rita and Riley were still chatting with each other when they were interrupted by a woman wearing a suit, standing before their holding cells.

"Hello," she said, addressing them both. "I'm Assistant District Attorney Janice Malone."

"Oh my gosh," Rita said under her breath, a knot forming in the pit of her stomach.

Riley leaned over and put her head in her hands, trying not to cry.

"Look, I just got off the phone with the store manager. The company is not pressing charges since the incident occurred outside and no merchandise was damaged."

Both Rita and Riley let out an audible sigh of relief.

Riley put her palms together, looked up toward the heavens, and mouthed, "Thank you," under her mask.

"So, unless either of you is going to press charges," ADA Malone continued, "you're free to go. Do either of you want to press charges against the other?"

Without looking at each other, both women shook their heads.

"All right," ADA Malone said. "But, ladies, before I let you go, there's something I want to say."

Both women gave her their full attention.

"Rita, you're not the police of everyone else. Riley, these are the rules, and they are here to protect you. Rita, you blame people like Riley for the government having to put restrictions on everyone. Riley, you blame people like Rita for allowing the government to put these restrictions on everyone.

"But here's the thing: we've all been affected by the pandemic, even if in completely different ways. We're all angry that this happened to us, feeling sorry for ourselves, and frustrated with the situation.

"Don't take it out on each other. We all want to defeat the virus and get our lives back. We all want this to end, even if we don't agree on the method. We need to get through this as painlessly as possible by not adding to each other's misery. Every person you encounter is already fighting the enemy of the pandemic. Don't add to their list of enemies by making yourself something they have to fight, too, okay?"

"Yes, ma'am," Rita and Riley said in unison.

"So, please," ADA Malone continued, "next time, before you go out in public—or before any time you're about to interact with someone—just take a moment to ask yourself how you're doing.

And next time you encounter someone who is as frustrated with the situation as you are, remember they're under the stress of the pandemic, too. Now more than ever, you know that every person you interact with is going through a tough time. And everyone deals with fear and anxiety in their own unique way. So have some compassion, okay? Not only for your fellow human beings, but for yourselves as well. Remember that, like everyone else, you're doing the best you can. And you're doing a great job of it. You're alive, you're still functioning, and you still have your jobs, your family, and your health."

Both Rita and Riley nodded in agreement.

"Listen," ADA Malone continued, "we've reached the homestretch. Even if we don't know how long the rest of the tunnel is, we can see the light at the end of it. Vaccines are ready, and they'll be available for everyone before we know it. We just have to hold out a little bit longer, okay?"

"Okay," both Rita and Riley said.

"Okay," ADA Malone said with finality as she motioned to the guard to unlock their cells.

As the women stepped out, ADA Malone held out a sheet of paper to each of them.

"This is a list of mental health services available to you, should you need any additional help in coping with this pandemic. I cannot stress enough how much I encourage you to look into them. It's really important that you take care of yourself, not just your physical health but your mental wellbeing, too."

"Thank you," Rita said as she took one of the sheets.

"Thank you," Riley also said, taking the other sheet.

"Have a good day, ladies," ADA Malone said. "I don't want to see you here again."

"You won't," said Rita.

As they both followed an officer back to the lobby—maintaining a generous six feet of distance from the officer and from each other—Riley said, "What a nerve-racking day."

"What a nerve-racking *year*," Rita replied.

Riley agreed, saying, "A nerve-racking year, indeed."

Epilogue

Once she was in the back seat, Riley asked her rideshare driver, "Is it okay if I roll my window up just a bit? I won't raise it above my chin."

"Yes, ma'am," her driver answered. "I'll roll the front passenger window up a little, too, if that helps. But I'll keep the ones on my side of the car all the way down, if that's okay with you."

"Yes, that will be fine," Riley replied.

As the car drove away from the police station, Riley pulled out her phone and started shopping for a new coat. All her winter coats were too big and heavy to bring along with her on shopping trips, but if windows were going to be down, then she needed a coat that was light enough that she could stuff it into a bag when she didn't need it but still warm enough so she wouldn't freeze in these window-down car rides.

She depended on rideshare drivers to take her places, and they depended on customers so they could still have a job. And they both depended on each other to feel safe: she did not want them to quit because they didn't feel safe being exposed to so many people in such a confined space; they did not want customers to quit requesting rides for the same reason. So, she understood now why the company had their rules. For everyone to feel safe and so there would be no fights, discussions, debates, or confusion: windows would be down, and masks would be worn. Same for stores and everywhere else—for now, until a better solution replaced this one.

She would not let up on being vigilant to make sure the government did not overstep the bounds of freedom, but she understood now that these restrictions were temporary (she would make sure of that) because this was the solution society had come up with to make sure that everyone felt comfortable going out in public.

Then, with that thought, she opened the text from Rita, clicked on the link she had sent, and started shopping for masks. After less than a minute of looking through the various colors and designs, Riley had already found a few that were just her style.

*   *   *

On her way home from the police station, Rita received a text from Riley.

"We've already gone viral," the text message read. "Do you want to join me in a video interview with channel two news later?"

Rita looked at the photo Riley had attached, a screenshot from one of the many videos that had already been shared on social media and various news sites. Rita cringed when she saw it. In the photo, she was unrecognizable. And now that she had gotten to know Riley, she saw in the photo a woman far different from the one she had talked with at the police station.

As she was looking at it, thinking of her shame, she received another text from Riley: "I thought we could show the world that we worked through our differences and tell them it's better to communicate than lash out. Also to remind people to check in with themselves and make sure they're mentally stable before going out so they don't blow up at strangers in public."

Rita laughed under her breath and responded, "Yes, I think that would be great. I'll call you in an hour after I get settled at home, and we can discuss our strategy."

She looked at the screenshot again, this time laughing when she saw the contorted expression on her face and her hand wildly spraying disinfectant into the air in all directions.

What a mess this whole thing has been, she thought. *For everyone.*

Interrupting her thoughts, her rideshare driver asked, "Ma'am, is it okay with you if I roll my window up just a bit? I've been driving for hours, and even with the heat on high, a scarf, a hat, and a coat, I am freezing. I'm afraid it will impact my driving. I can cancel the ride and drop you off somewhere, if you'd prefer."

"No, that's all right," Rita replied. "How about I keep my window down all the way, but you can roll the other three up one third of the way?"

"That works for me," her driver said. "I'm glad we could come to an agreement. You know, we all just want to feel safe."

With her head out the window, Rita sighed and said, "I know."

Author's Note

As ADA Malone said, this pandemic has affected everyone differently, and as a result we each have a unique perspective on a globally shared event. How has the SARS-CoV-2 pandemic affected you personally? What changes have you had to make? How did you cope? For me, I write. Maybe you paint, draw, or sculpt. Maybe you create music. Maybe you also write, be it song lyrics, a forum comment, a blog post, a memoir, or even a fictional story. Whatever the case, I encourage you to share your unique experience in the way which most suits you. We can all benefit from learning about how this pandemic has affected each of us so we can grow together and feel a sense of community in a time when we feel physically and emotionally isolated.

On a personal note, I'd like to extend my sincerest sympathies to all of you who have lost dear loved ones to COVID-19 in one way or another. While this story was intended to be a comedy that would entertain for a couple of hours, if not also provide a sense of comfort and to let people know they are not alone, the effects of this pandemic are serious and are not to be taken lightly. Please take care of yourself, both physically and mentally, and ask others how you can help them take care of themselves, too. You might be surprised at just how much helping someone else can bring you joy and a sense of community, especially in a time when we feel disconnected.

Since this pandemic began and the stay-at-home orders were put in place, mental health resources have become available specifically for addressing the effects of the restrictions and other pandemic-related stressors. Please take a moment to find local resources available to you, even if you do not need them now, so you will be familiar with them if you or a loved one is in need in the future. In the United States, the CDC and HHS both have a list of national resources and suggestions for coping with stress during a pandemic. These resources can be found at:

https://www.cdc.gov/coronavirus/2019-ncov/daily-life-coping/managing-stress-anxiety.html

and

https://www.hhs.gov/coronavirus/mental-health-and-coping/index.html.

Although we are physically distanced, we are not alone.

Novella Jean

December 10, 2020

Acknowledgements

To my Mom, my Aunt Glenda, and my sister Robin: thank you for your inspiration, your support, and all the laughter.

To my girls, Rachel, Sarah, Jodi, Kate, and Candice: Our group texts have done more than you know to keep me sane during this year. Thank you for bringing laughter, thoughtful discussions, and a sense of community into my home over two thousand miles away.

And to my husband, Tim: I am so fortunate that I got stuck in lockdown with you.